Word List

Here is a list of words that might make it easier to read this book. You'll find them in boldface the first time they appear in the story.

habitat	HA-buh-tat
veterinarian	ve-tuh-ruh-NAIR-ee-uhn
stomachache	STUM-uhk-ayk
nutritionist	noo-TRI-shuh-nist
examine	ig-ZA-min
behaviorist	bi-HAYV-yer-ist
architect	AR-kuh-tekt
conditioners	kuhn-DI-shuh-nerz
microscope	MY-kruh-skohp
personality	per-suh-NAL-uh-tee
temperature	TEM-per-uh-cher
pistachio	puh-STA-shee-oh

Barbie™

The Giant Panda Problem

© 1998 Mattel, Inc. Barbie and associated trademarks are owned and used under license from Mattel, Inc. All Rights Reserved. Published by Grolier Enterprises, Inc. Story by Karen Stillman. Photo crew: Scott Fujikawa, Romona Yoh, James La Bianca, Greg Roccia, Jeffrey Fiterman, and Judy Tsuno. Produced by Bumpy Slide Books. Printed in the United States of America.

ISBN: 0-7172-8824-2

Grolier Books

It was early morning at the zoo where Barbie worked. The sun was just beginning to warm the four gorillas in their **habitat.**

Barbie stepped closer to the animals and smiled. The oldest gorilla was sitting in the grass eating bananas. "Good morning, Bongo," she said. "You look much better today."

The gorilla stopped chewing. He looked at Barbie and grunted loudly. Then he went right back to his breakfast.

Barbie laughed. She loved being a **veterinarian** at the zoo. But she always worried when one of the animals was sick. The night before, Bongo had had a **stomachache.** Barbie had given the gorilla some medicine to make him feel better. Now she was very glad to see that it had helped.

Just then, Barbie heard a friendly voice. "Hi, Barbie. I've been looking for you!"

Barbie smiled when she saw that it was Christie. Christie was the zoo's **nutritionist.** Her job was to decide what foods to feed the animals.

"Good morning," Barbie replied.

"Bongo looks much better," said Christie.

They turned to watch him. Then the gorilla threw a banana up in the air and caught it. Barbie and Christie laughed.

"He must be feeling better," added Barbie. "He's up to his old tricks."

"Well, I'm glad, because we have to hurry," Christie told her. "Dr. Livingston wants to see us in his office right away!"

Dr. Livingston was in charge of the zoo,

and he was their boss.

"I hope nothing's wrong," said Barbie.

"I know. Me, too," Christie agreed.

Barbie and Christie climbed into the zoo's special truck. The truck was like a hospital on wheels. In the back were instruments Barbie used to **examine** sick animals. Next to the instruments were boxes full of different kinds of medicine.

First, Barbie and Christie drove past the giraffes. A new baby giraffe had been born only a few weeks before. This morning he was staying close to his mother. The baby followed a few steps behind as his mother walked from one end of their habitat to the other.

Next the truck passed the seal pool. A seal named Jack was resting on a rock in the sun. Another seal, named Jill, waddled over to the water. Just as the truck drove past, Jill slid into the water and started swimming.

Finally Barbie and Christie reached the

building. Dr. Livingston's office was a small room with photographs of animals on the walls.

"Come in," said Dr. Livingston. He always wore a white shirt and a tie. Everyone loved his ties. They never had stripes or dots. Instead, each tie was covered with tiny animals. Barbie smiled when she saw the tie he was wearing today. It had little lions all over it.

The two friends stepped into Dr. Livingston's office. They were surprised to find Ken already there. Ken worked as a **behaviorist** at the zoo. His job was to study how all the animals acted. He knew which animals liked to play a lot and which ones were quiet and shy.

"Please sit down," said their boss.

"You haven't called all of us into your office in a long time," said Barbie, taking a seat. "There must be something very important going on."

"Yes, there is," Dr. Livingston replied. "As you already know, the zoo will soon be getting a pair of giant pandas named Pan and Lang-Lang from China."

"I can't wait to study them!" Barbie said quickly. "They're such wonderful animals."

"I'm glad to hear that, Barbie," said Dr. Livingston, "because it looks like you may be getting a chance to study them sooner than you think."

"What do you mean?" asked Barbie. "I thought they were coming in two months."

Dr. Livingston explained, "Well, today I found out that our new pandas will be arriving one month earlier than we expected."

"That means we have to get everything ready by next month!" said Ken. "Can it be done?"

Christie spoke up. "We should have food by then. Pandas eat nothing but bamboo. A nutritionist in China sent me a list of the types of bamboo that Pan and Lang-Lang like to eat. I've already started growing them. What about the pandas' new home?"

"As you know, I've hired a zoo **architect** to design and build the habitats for the pandas," said Dr. Livingston. "But the habitats are only half finished. Now we'll really have to rush to have them ready in time."

"Is there anything we can do to help?" Barbie asked.

"Actually, there is," said Dr. Livingston. "I have to go to Africa for the rest of the month on business. So I won't be here when the pandas arrive. Barbie, I'd like to put you in charge of the panda project. Do you think you can handle it?"

Barbie was happily surprised. Dr. Livingston had never put her in charge of such a big project before. "Thank you," she said. "Yes, I think I can handle it." Then she turned to Christie and Ken. "If you two will help me," she said.

"Of course!" Christie answered.

"You bet!" Ken replied.

"Wonderful!" Dr. Livingston said with a smile.

Just then the door opened. A young Asian woman with long, black hair stepped in. "Am I late?" she asked.

"No, Su, you're right on time," said Dr. Livingston. He stood up. "Everybody, this is Miss Chong Tan Su. She works for a group in China that protects pandas from harm. She has visited Pan and Lang-Lang often in China. She's come here to help us make sure they'll be happy and healthy in their new home."

Dr. Livingston introduced his staff.

"It's nice to meet you, Miss Su," said Ken, shaking her hand.

"Thank you," she replied. "Actually, *Su* is my first name. In China, your first name comes last. So, please, call me Su."

Barbie and Christie both smiled and shook Su's hand.

"I'm looking forward to working with all of you," said Su. "I'm sure that you'll do your best to give Pan and Lang-Lang a good home."

"You can count on it!" said Barbie. "We can't wait to meet our two new zoo guests."

"Why don't we go look at their habitats?" said Ken. "That way we'll be able to see how much work needs to be done."

"Great idea!" said Christie.

"Good," said Dr. Livingston. "The architect is already over there."

Everyone started to leave.

"Just a minute, Barbie," Dr. Livingston called. "I need to discuss one more thing with you before you go."

Barbie stepped back into the office and sat down.

"Barbie," he began, "there's something more you should know about this project."

Chapter Two

Dr. Livingston sat down across from Barbie. "I put you in charge of the panda project because I know you'll do a great job," he told her. "I'm worried, though. Not many zoos have pandas. That means that when Pan and Lang-Lang get here, a lot of reporters will come here, too. They'll all want to write news stories about the pandas. And photographers will want to take pictures of them."

"I guess the whole world will be watching to see how the pandas like their new home," said Barbie.

"That's right," said Dr. Livingston. "And you'll be in charge of them. That means the whole world will be watching you, too."

Barbie thought for a moment. "I understand," she replied. "I'll try to be ready for anything."

"You always are, Barbie," Dr. Livingston told her. "The zoo is very lucky to have you."

"Thank you," said Barbie. She was a little worried, but mostly excited. She knew the entire zoo staff wanted Pan and Lang-Lang to be happy in their new home.

Barbie headed off to the area of the zoo where the pandas' habitats were being built. There, Ken, Christie, and Su were already speaking with Dan, the architect.

"I'm building a separate habitat for each animal because I know that pandas like to live alone," Dan told them. "Let me take you through one of them."

Dan started in the front yard of one of the habitats. The space was empty because no trees or shrubs had been planted yet.

"When the pandas are here, zoo visitors will be able to watch them," Dan explained. He took them through a tunnel that led to two more rooms. "One of these rooms will be a backyard," he said. "The other will be a special sleeping area. When the pandas are in these two places, zoo visitors won't be able to see them at all."

Barbie thought for a moment. "So, at first, we will keep them in their backyards and sleeping areas."

"Right," agreed Ken. "Pan and Lang-Lang will be very tired from their trip. They'll need some time to get used to their new surroundings. We shouldn't let zoo visitors see the pandas until we know the animals are comfortable."

"As you can see, there's nothing in the habitats now," said Dan. "I have some plans, but let's make sure we have thought of everything the pandas will need."

"Well, pandas like to climb," Ken pointed

out. "And they like to wade in water, but only up to their ankles."

"Great! I already plan to include trees, logs, and shallow ponds," Dan said, checking his notes.

"I brought photos of Pan and Lang-Lang in their habitats in China," offered Su. "Perhaps the photos will give you some ideas."

"Thanks," replied Dan. "I'll look them over." Then he thought for a moment. "In the plans, the habitats look exactly alike. Is that okay?" he asked.

"That's a good question," said Barbie. She turned to Su. "Su, can you tell us anything about Pan and Lang-Lang? What do they like? Would one prefer more ponds or more trees?"

"Well, Pan is very shy and hardly ever exercises," explained Su. "In China she likes mostly to lie in her pond. But Lang-Lang loves to climb and play."

"Then let's put an extra pond in Pan's habitat and add more trees and logs to Lang-Lang's habitat," suggested Ken.

"That sounds good," said Su.

Dan continued to read from his notes. "It's much warmer here than it is in China. Should the sleeping areas have air **conditioners**?"

"That's a great idea!" Barbie and Su said at the same time. They looked at each other and smiled.

"Wow, even my apartment doesn't have an air conditioner!" joked Ken.

"It might if you were a panda!" replied Christie. Everyone laughed.

The next few weeks were busy for everyone. Barbie, Su, and Ken worked with Dan to make sure the habitats were ready in time. And Christie made sure that there would be plenty of fresh bamboo.

One day, Barbie took some time out to talk to a group of students visiting the zoo. A few of them asked about the giraffes and the lions, but most of them wanted to know about Pan and Lang-Lang. Their teacher had told them the two giant pandas would be coming to live at the zoo very soon. He also had told the class it would be doing a project on the pandas. The students were very excited and asked Barbie a lot of questions.

"What do pandas eat?" asked a girl with long, black braids.

"How old are they?" asked a boy with freckles.

"Can we pet them?" asked a girl in a pink sweater.

Barbie laughed. "One question at a time, okay? Pandas eat different kinds of bamboo. We're growing some here, in special areas of the zoo. Pan and Lang-Lang are four years old. And, no, you can't pet them. Don't forget that these are wild animals, not pets. They can be dangerous. It's important that we respect them and all wild animals."

Barbie finished answering everyone's questions. The teacher thanked her as they left.

A few days later, the students sent Barbie

two big signs. One read *Welcome Pan* and the other said *Welcome Lang-Lang* in bright yellow letters. Barbie thought the signs were wonderful. She hung both signs right in front of the pandas' habitats.

Finally the big day arrived. Reporters and photographers had been waiting in front of the panda habitats for hours to see the newcomers. At last the truck carrying Pan and Lang-Lang appeared. The pandas made honking sounds as the truck came to a stop outside the habitats. Barbie laughed. It was as though the pandas were saying hello to everyone.

Click! Click! Barbie heard the sound of cameras. She turned and saw photographers taking pictures of Pan's and Lang-Lang's crates as they were carefully taken off the truck. Reporters were busy writing on their notepads.

"Doctor!" called a reporter. "I know that you're in charge of the panda project. I'd like to ask you some questions."

"I'd be happy to talk to you," said Barbie. "But first, Miss Chong and I have to check on the pandas."

"May we come with you?" asked the reporter.

Barbie smiled but shook her head. "I'm sorry. Only zoo workers can go into the pandas' backyards."

Barbie and Su quietly went into the backyard area where the crates had been taken. Then the crates were carefully opened, and the pandas were free to explore.

Barbie and Su looked at Pan first. Barbie was thrilled. She had never seen a panda up close.

Pan was very big. She had thick, white fur on her face and large, black eyes with black patches around them.

"She's beautiful!" whispered Barbie.

Barbie watched as Pan climbed onto one of the logs and sniffed a nearby tree. Then she waded into her pond, sniffing around some more.

"She's really exploring," said Barbie. "I thought that Pan was usually quiet and shy."

"She is!" said Su. "I've never seen her so playful. She must be glad to be out of her crate."

Barbie and Su then walked to Lang-Lang's habitat and were surprised by what they saw. The panda was sitting quietly in a corner of the backyard. Lang-Lang looked just like Pan, but he wasn't eating or playing or climbing.

"That's strange," said Su. "In China, Lang-Lang was very active and curious."

"He's probably tired from his trip," said Barbie. She looked at the panda again. He lowered his head and leaned against the habitat wall. "I don't think there's anything to worry about." Then Barbie added, "But we'll keep an eye on him, just in case."

Chapter Three

The next day was Sunday. Barbie invited Su, Christie, and Ken to her house for dinner. "Let's celebrate the pandas' arrival," she said. "And we can also thank Su for helping us get ready for them. We'll cook a traditional American meal."

Su smiled. "Thank you. That sounds like fun," she said. "I love hamburgers and apple pie."

Barbie grinned. "There are lots of different traditional American foods. Hamburgers and apple pie are certainly among them. But that's not exactly what I had in mind. I think you'll like our meal, though. See you at eight o'clock, then?"

"I'll be there!" replied Su.

Barbie's friends arrived at her house right on time. She opened the door and welcomed them to her home.

"I hope you're all hungry," said Barbie. "There's plenty of food!"

"Mmm! Something smells great!" said Ken.

Everyone sat down at the table, and Barbie began to serve the meal. She brought out turkey with stuffing, green beans, mashed potatoes and gravy, cranberry sauce, and homemade bread. For dessert, Ken had made a chocolate cake.

Everyone agreed that the food was delicious! Su ate three helpings of turkey, and Ken had two pieces of chocolate cake.

When the group was finished, Su smiled and stretched. "That was great, Barbie!" she said. "Thank you very much. So that was a traditional American meal?"

Barbie nodded. "Probably the most traditional:

It's what we eat on Thanksgiving," she said.

"But Americans eat all sorts of things," added Christie.

"Yes," Ken agreed. "We eat spaghetti, fried chicken, tacos, meat loaf, pizza, and—gee, I think I'm getting hungry again."

Everyone laughed.

"Do the Chinese have many different types of foods, too?" Barbie asked Su.

"China is very big," replied Su. "People eat various foods all over the country. But there are some traditional dishes that are common to many Chinese. As soon as Pan and Lang-Lang are settled, I have to go back to China. But if you like, I can teach you how to cook a traditional Chinese meal before I leave."

"That would be great!" said Barbie.

Su leaned back and sighed, patting her full stomach. "Well, I hope Pan and Lang-Lang like America as much as I do!" she said.

First thing Monday morning, the four friends went to check on the pandas. It was a very hot day. Pan was lying on her belly in her cool pond.

Christie put some fresh bamboo in Pan's habitat. The panda began munching on it at once.

"She seems very happy," said Barbie. "Let's go check on Lang-Lang."

When they reached Lang-Lang's habitat, Christie gave him some bamboo. Lang-Lang picked it up and sniffed it. But then, instead of taking a bite, he dropped the stem and slowly walked away. When he got to the habitat's back wall, Lang-Lang sat down and closed his eyes.

"Something's definitely wrong," said Su. She turned to Christie. "Could there be a problem with Lang-Lang's food?"

"Well," said Christie, "pandas are very picky when it comes to food. But I'm feeding them the kinds of bamboo they ate in China. I make sure it's all fresh and clean. I know they won't eat bamboo that doesn't look or smell good. And I wash it a lot because I know they prefer their food wet."

"It sounds as if you're doing all the right things," said Barbie.

Christie picked up Lang-Lang's bamboo and looked at it. "I think I'll check it under the **microscope** just to make sure I didn't miss anything. I'll be back in a few minutes."

She took the bamboo back to her office. There, Christie examined every inch of the bamboo under the microscope. When she was sure that there was nothing unusual about it, she carefully rinsed it again. Then she brought it back to Lang-Lang's habitat.

The four friends watched as the panda smelled the bamboo. Then he walked away.

Christie looked down. "I'm not sure what else to do."

"Maybe it's not the food," Barbie said gently.

Su sighed. Barbie could see that she was upset. And although she didn't want to alarm Su, Barbie was starting to worry, too.

"What will happen if Lang-Lang doesn't start to eat soon?" Su asked in a nervous voice.

This thought was on everyone's mind.

Barbie spoke quietly. "Well, as long as he's drinking, a large animal like him can go for a while without eating. But if he gets too weak, we'll have to take him to the hospital and feed him through a tube."

"Oh, dear," said Su.

"It won't come to that," said Barbie. "We won't give up until we figure out what the problem is." She put her arm around her new friend and thought, "I just hope we find it soon."

Chapter Four

Barbie, Su, Christie, and Ken were standing in Lang-Lang's habitat. The panda had fallen asleep sitting against a tree.

"Do you think we should call Dr. Livingston?" asked Christie.

"No, not yet," said Barbie. "Let's first try to solve this problem ourselves. If things aren't better by next Monday, I'll call him in Africa."

Suddenly Ken had an idea. "Maybe it's the heat," he said. "Remember, it's much warmer here than it is in China. Animals often stop eating and playing when they're hot."

"That's a good point," said Christie. "But Lang-Lang has trees for shade. He can wade into his pond, and there's an air conditioner where he sleeps. What else can we do to make it cooler?"

"Sometimes on hot days I wish that I could just lie down on a block of ice," said Ken.

"That's it!" Barbie exclaimed. "We could make a huge block of ice for Lang-Lang!"

"How?" Christie wondered.

"Follow me," said Barbie.

Barbie led them to a zoo supply room. There she found a new, green garbage can. She rolled it into one of the zoo's walk-in freezers. The freezer was full of frozen meat and fish for the animals. Barbie began to fill the garbage can with water from a hose.

"I see," said Ken. "The garbage can is like a huge ice cube tray!"

"Why don't I put some pieces of bamboo in the water?" Christie suggested. "The bamboo will freeze into the ice. When the ice starts to melt, maybe Lang-Lang will eat the ice-cold pieces."

"Good thinking, Christie!" said Barbie.

It took a whole day for the water to freeze. When it finally did, the group dragged the heavy garbage can to the panda's habitat. In Lang-Lang's backyard, they ran water over the can to loosen the ice. Then they emptied the block onto the grass.

At first, Lang-Lang just looked at the ice. But then he tapped it with his paw and rubbed up against it. Then he even tried to climb on top of it!

"I think Lang-Lang likes it," said Su.

"I do, too," Ken agreed. "Maybe now that he's cooler, he'll eat."

After a few minutes, Lang-Lang reached his paw into the melting ice and pulled out a piece of bamboo near the top. Then he bit into it. But instead of eating the bamboo, he tossed it aside.

Everyone sighed at the same time.

"That was a good guess," said Barbie. "It just

wasn't the right answer. But let's keep thinking. We're bound to find the solution."

Suddenly Ken jumped up. "Wait a minute!" he said excitedly. "Maybe the problem isn't the heat. Maybe it's the habitat!"

"What do you mean?" asked Su.

"Well, sometimes an animal will stop eating when it isn't happy in its home," said Ken.

"But we tried to have everything in the habitat that we thought Lang-Lang would like," said Christie.

"That's true," said Ken. "But maybe it just doesn't feel like home." He pulled a photograph out of his bag. "This is the picture of Lang-Lang's habitat in China that Su gave Dan. Let's see. The trees are closer together than they are in his habitat here. And there are more ponds."

"I see what you're saying," said Christie. "You want us to make his home here look just like the one in China!"

"Exactly!" said Ken. "I'll call the architect right now."

"I hope this works," said Su. "If it doesn't, I wonder if I should make plans to take Lang-Lang back to China."

Barbie thought for a moment. "Lang-Lang's already tired and a bit weak. The long trip back to China might make him worse," she said.

"I hadn't thought of that," said Su. "But I feel like I should do something. What will happen if this doesn't work?"

Barbie explained, "Well, I'll have to give Lang-Lang a shot that will make him sleep for a while. Then I can examine him. But I don't want to do that until we've tried everything."

"It's just so hard to wait," Su said softly.

"I know," agreed Barbie. "Su, it will take Dan and his crew some time to rearrange the habitat. I have to check on some of the other animals. Ken and Christie will be here watching

Lang-Lang. Why don't you come with me? It will take your mind off things."

Su thought for a moment. "Okay," she agreed.

Barbie and Su climbed into Barbie's truck. Their first stop was to see a young elephant, named Fluffy, who was munching on some hay.

"Fluffy needs special vitamins," said Barbie. "For a while, every time I tried to give them to her, she spit them out. So one day I decided to hide the vitamins in a piece of sugarcane."

"That was a good idea," said Su.

Next, Barbie and Su stopped by the zoo's animal hospital. There they visited a lion cub, named Ella.

"What's wrong with Ella?" asked Su.

"Her mother can't feed her," said Barbie.

"Meow," whined Ella.

Su laughed and said, "She sounds just like a house cat."

Barbie took Ella in her arms and fed her milk

from a bottle like a baby. Su watched as the lion cub drank every last drop.

"You were one hungry cub!" said Barbie, scratching Ella's belly. Ella playfully reached for Barbie with her paw.

Barbie and Su said good-bye to Ella and drove back to see Lang-Lang's habitat. They both hoped that it had been rearranged by now and that they'd find the panda munching on some bamboo.

But when they reached the front of Lang-Lang's habitat, Barbie and Su found something that neither of them had expected to see.

Chapter Five

A man wearing a sweater and tie was holding a microphone. He was talking to a woman holding a television camera. Barbie knew the man was a television reporter. She saw him every night on the evening news.

Barbie and Su jumped out of Barbie's truck. "What are they doing here?" asked Su.

"I'll find out," said Barbie. "Maybe you can check and see how the habitat is coming along."

"All right," said Su.

The reporter and the camerawoman saw Barbie and hurried toward her.

"Excuse me, Doctor," said the reporter. "I'm doing a report for the evening news. May I talk to you about the pandas?"

Barbie smiled and nodded her head. "Of course. I'd be happy to answer any questions about Pan and Lang-Lang."

"We've heard that Lang-Lang is sick," said the reporter into the microphone. "Is that true?"

The camerawoman moved closer to Barbie. At first, Barbie wasn't sure what to say. The zoo was taking good care of the pandas. But people might not think so if they thought Lang-Lang was sick. Should she tell the reporter the truth? She took a deep breath.

"We're not sure," Barbie answered honestly. "We are watching Lang-Lang very carefully. Sometimes it takes time for an animal to get used to a new home."

"But we've heard that Pan is doing just fine," the reporter said.

"Yes, that's true," said Barbie. "But, like people, animals are not all the same. Each panda has its own **personality.** And it might just be that Lang-Lang is taking longer to adjust."

The reporter had other questions for Barbie. She answered them all as best she could. Finally he thanked her and left. Then Barbie went over to Lang-Lang's habitat. There she saw Dan planting one last tree. Su was standing with Christie and Ken.

"This is amazing," said Su. "The habitat looks just like the one in China."

It wasn't long before everyone was watching Lang-Lang pick up a piece of bamboo and begin chomping on it.

"Do you think he's going to eat it?" Su asked hopefully.

But before Su finished speaking, Lang-Lang threw the bamboo down on the ground and then slumped against the wall.

"Oh, Lang-Lang!" pleaded Su. "Why won't you eat?"

Just then, Barbie looked on the ground and saw another piece of bamboo that Lang-Lang had tossed aside. She picked it up and looked at it very closely. "I think I just found a clue," she said. "There are teeth marks on this piece, too. Lang-Lang started to bite it but stopped. I wonder if he wants to eat but can't."

"What do you mean?" asked Su.

"Maybe Lang-Lang has a toothache," suggested Barbie.

"Of course!" said Christie. "Sometimes when an animal's tooth hurts, it will just stop eating."

"To find out, I'll have to look inside his mouth," Barbie explained. "I can't do that alone, so I will call the animal hospital. Then another veterinarian will come and help. We'll also give him a complete checkup. I hate to do this, but I have no choice."

Two days later, Barbie and a veterinarian named Steve Woodward entered Lang-Lang's habitat. Steve gave Lang-Lang a shot to make him sleep. With the panda quiet and still, Barbie and Steve would be able to look at him more closely.

"Sweet dreams, Lang-Lang," said Barbie softly to the panda.

When they were sure the panda was in a deep sleep, Barbie and Steve opened the animal's mouth and checked inside.

"All his teeth look healthy," said Barbie.

"What's this?" asked Steve. He reached into Lang-Lang's mouth and pulled out a tiny piece of bamboo.

"It must have gotten caught between two of his teeth," Barbie concluded. "This piece of bamboo is sharp. It may have made it painful for Lang-Lang to chew."

"Let's finish his checkup," said Steve. "We'll know if that was the problem when he wakes up."

Barbie took Lang-Lang's **temperature** and listened to his heart. Steve felt the panda's fur and muscles. He wanted to make sure Lang-Lang hadn't gotten any bumps or cuts on the trip over from China.

"Everything else seems to be fine," said Steve. "I hope he'll eat now."

"Me, too," said Barbie. She looked tenderly at Lang-Lang. "You know, I love my job. But sometimes I think that being a veterinarian is harder than being a people doctor. Most of the time, people can tell you what is hurting them. Animals can't do that. So a vet needs to look for clues."

Soon it was nighttime. Everyone was hungry and tired, but no one wanted to leave Lang-Lang.

Su walked over to Lang-Lang. She bent down and petted the sleeping panda. She spoke to him softly in Chinese.

"Don't worry, Su," Barbie told her friend. "If the bamboo stuck between his teeth isn't the

problem, we'll find out what is."

"Thank you, Barbie," said Su, trying to smile.

"You know, tomorrow's Friday," Christie said to Barbie. "If Lang-Lang's not better soon, we're going to have to call Dr. Livingston back from Africa. Then we'll need to take the panda to the hospital."

"I know. But we still have a little time left," said Barbie. Then she snapped her fingers. "Wait a minute! I just thought of one more thing we can do."

Chapter Six

"What is it?" asked Ken.

Barbie explained. "There are many more zoos with pandas in China than there are here. Maybe one of them has had the same problem. If we could contact a veterinarian at a Chinese zoo, we might be able to find an answer."

"I know someone back home who works in a zoo," said Su. "Why don't we e-mail him?"

"Terrific idea!" said Barbie.

Barbie and Su went to Barbie's office. Just like Dr. Livingston, Barbie had animal photos everywhere. Barbie turned on her computer and logged onto the Internet. Then Su typed in the e-mail address of the veterinarian in China. She wrote to him about Lang-Lang's problem and asked for help.

"I hope he has the answer," worried Su.

After waiting a while, Barbie said, "Let's all go home and check back tomorrow. There's nothing more we can do now but wait."

Around lunchtime the next day, Barbie, Christie, and Su checked on Lang-Lang. They watched as the panda opened his eyes and yawned. Christie had put some bamboo close to him, but instead of eating it, he began to make noise.

"Honk! Honk!" called Lang-Lang.

"I wonder what he's saying," said Christie.

"I think he's telling us that he needs help," said Barbie.

Lang-Lang kept honking, but he still didn't eat. Su sighed. "I guess it wasn't his teeth."

"Don't give up hope, Su," Barbie told her.

"Let's go to my office and see if your friend has answered our e-mail."

When the three women got to Barbie's office, Ken was there.

"Hey, guys!" said Ken. "I brought something to cheer you up." He reached into a bag and pulled out a carton of strawberry ice cream and four bowls.

"Ice cream!" said Su.

"And sprinkles!" Ken added as he pulled a jar of them out of the bag.

Barbie smiled. "What a sweet thing to do!"

"I just wish I could do more," said Ken as he began scooping the ice cream into the bowls.

Just then, Su looked at Barbie's computer.

"Barbie!" cried Su. "My veterinarian friend in China answered our e-mail. It says, 'It sounds like you're doing all the right things. I don't know how to help. But remember that sometimes the answer is right under your nose.'"

"That's an unusual e-mail," commented Ken.

He handed bowls of ice cream to Su, Christie, and Barbie. Christie poured on the sprinkles.

Barbie lifted the spoon to her mouth, then stopped and turned to Ken. "I'm surprised that you brought us strawberry ice cream, Ken," she said. "I thought that your favorite flavor was chocolate."

"It is. But I ate two chocolate bars yesterday, the rest of that chocolate cake from dinner at your house, and a chocolate doughnut this morning," Ken explained. "I'm in the mood for something different."

Barbie, Christie, and Su put down their spoons at the same time. They all looked at one another. Then they looked at Ken.

"What's the matter?" Ken asked.

"Ken," said Barbie, "I think you may have just solved Lang-Lang's problem!"

"I don't understand," said Ken, scratching his head. "Does he like ice cream, too?"

"Ken, you like chocolate, right?" Barbie

began. "But you said that you've been eating a lot of it lately and that you'd like something *different.* Maybe Lang-Lang is feeling the same way. Maybe he's tired of eating the same kind of bamboo and just wants something different!"

Christie jumped up. "Pandas in captivity eat nine different kinds of bamboo," she said. "Lang-Lang only ate four of those kinds in China, so that's what we've been trying to feed him. But remember that pandas can be very picky eaters. Maybe he's tired of those four types of bamboo. Let's see if he'll eat one of the other kinds."

"Do we have any of them here?" Ken asked.

Christie shook her head. "No, but I know where I can get some."

Christie called another zoo that grew bamboo for their animals. The nutritionist there told Christie that the zoo had all five kinds of bamboo she needed. She said that she would send some to Christie right away.

The next day, the zoo staff couldn't wait for the shipment to arrive. When the box was opened, Christie looked at the bamboo carefully. She cleaned it, chopped it into pieces, and wet it. Everyone watched as she put it in Lang-Lang's habitat.

The panda was just waking up. He moved toward the bamboo and picked up a stem. He sniffed it, then took a tiny bite.

"Oh, I hope this works!" whispered Su.

Suddenly Lang-Lang took a big bite of the new bamboo. He chomped until he had eaten the whole piece. Then he reached for another one.

"Hooray!" cried Christie.

"We did it!" exclaimed Barbie.

"I can't believe that the answer was so simple," said Ken.

"My friend in China was right," said Su. "Sometimes the answer *is* right under your nose."

The four friends turned to watch the pandas. Pan spent the afternoon rolling around on a big, yellow ball. Lang-Lang ate bamboo for hours. Then he climbed on every log and sniffed every tree in his habitat. As the sun set, Lang-Lang waded into his pond and lay down in the cool water.

"It's such a relief to see both pandas happy," said Su.

"It sure is," Barbie agreed. "Tomorrow we'll let them into the front yard so the zoo visitors can see them, too. I'll call that television reporter. I'll bet this is a story he'll want to report!"

Before they left, Ken took some pictures of the happy pandas.

That night, Su went to Barbie's house to cook dinner. Christie and Ken came, too. Su taught everyone how to cook a traditional Chinese meal.

With Su's help, Barbie, Christie, and Ken each cooked a different Chinese dish. Barbie used a kind of pan called a wok to stir-fry beef and bok choy, a green, leafy vegetable. Christie made fried rice. And Ken made sweet and sour soup.

"In China we usually eat with chopsticks," said Su as they all sat down at the table.

"Like this?" asked Christie, grabbing a piece of beef with her chopsticks.

"That's perfect!" replied Su.

Christie's piece of beef fell on the table. "Oops," she giggled.

"Keep trying," said Su. "You'll get it!"

Soon all of them were eating with chopsticks and talking about the meal. When at last the plates were empty, everyone helped clear the table.

"Now that both pandas are doing well, it's time for me to go back to China," Su announced.

"I'm glad that you're going to see your family and friends again," Barbie told her. "But we'll miss you, Su."

"I'll miss all of you, too," said Su. "I hope you'll come visit me in China someday."

"Me, too," said Barbie. Then she took a picture out of a bag. She handed it to Su and said,

"This is from all of us. We hope it will always remind you of your two favorite pandas."

It was the picture Ken had taken earlier in the day, in a bamboo frame. Su stared at the picture and then looked up with tears in her eyes. "Thank you so much," she said and hugged her friends.

"Now," Ken said, "how about dessert?"

Su frowned and explained, "Sorry, I didn't plan on dessert."

"No problem," replied Ken. "I *always* plan on dessert." He turned and opened the freezer.

Barbie groaned, "Oh, no. Not strawberry ice cream again!"

Ken explained, "Not *just* strawberry. I also brought chocolate, vanilla, **pistachio,** and mint chocolate chip. After all, you never know what you might be in the mood for!"

The four friends laughed. Then they all sat back down to enjoy their time—and their ice cream—together.